S0-BYC-628

Initial	Last Name, First Name	Z153112/2022	
Z	zielke,Heather		

Book Title	# of Items 1
the extra mile	Pickup

Gr/Subject OR Category
Literature Fiction
Early Elementary (K-2)

Item Number 0044

Full Price	Discount Price	
$1.00	$0.50	448625

The Extra Mile

Illustrated by
Laura Martin

A
SUNBEAM
BOOK

The Extra Mile

Written by Susan Schwartz

Rod and Staff Publishers, Inc.
P.O. Box 3, Hwy. 172
Crockett, Kentucky 41413
Telephone: 606-522-4348

Copyright 2010

By Rod and Staff Publishers, Inc.
Crockett, Kentucky 41413

Printed in U.S.A.

ISBN 978-07399-2423-5

Catalog no. 2699

2   3   4   5   6 —   21   20   19   18   17   16   15   14   13   12

Contents

1. The Extra Mile 11

2. The Missing Worksheet 16

3. Caught on the Fishing Line . . . 20

4. Marcus Builds Too 24

5. Matthew's Dollar Bill 28

6. A Good Patient 34

7. Grandmother's Helper 37

8. Time to Obey 42

9. Rachel Helps Her Sister 46

10. No More Stars 50

11. The Peach Decision 56

12. Recess Time for Eric 61

13. Playtime Troubles 66

14. A Letter for Grandmother 71

15. Keeping On and On 76

16. A Surprise for Sister Faith 82

17. Violet Shares Her

             Grandmother 88

18. Mrs. Palmer Forgets 92

19. Norma's Candy Cup 96

20. Rosanna's Father 102

21. A Little Extra Story Time . . . 107

22. Anson Forgets 111

23. Arithmetic Perseverance 117

24. Aunt Barbara Too? 121

25. Ellen's New Friend 127

26. Good, Better, Best. 132

27. Pitch and Catch 137

28. Aunt Rose Makes

    Tomato Soup 141

29. Ruby Describes 146

30. Sunshine Does Not

    Understand 150

31. Thank You, God, for Big

    Brothers. 154

32. The Damaged Bible 158

33. The One Side 163

34. The Other Side 167

35. Working for Money. 171

1

The Extra Mile

"Grandfather, let's go," eight-year-old Galen urged, tugging at Grandfather's arm.

"I'm ready," Grandfather answered. He loaded his chain saw on the cart that was hooked to the tractor.

Father, Galen, and six-year-old Mabel jumped onto the empty cart. Grandfather drove the tractor out the back lane that led to the woods.

"What a huge tree!" Galen exclaimed

when Grandfather shut off the tractor ignition. "It will make a lot of wood for you to burn this winter."

"Yes, it will," Grandfather agreed. "I hope it will dry out for a few months. Then we can use it later in the winter."

Father began to saw off the branches. After a while he called, "Galen, Mabel, you can stack all these smaller pieces on the cart."

Galen and Mabel came running. They were happy to help with Grandfather's wood. Back and forth they walked. They walked from the tree to the cart, and then from the cart to the tree. Back and forth. Back and forth. It took a long time to fill the cart.

When the cart was full, Father, Galen, and Mabel had to walk to the woodshed because there was no room to sit on the cart. Grandmother brought some

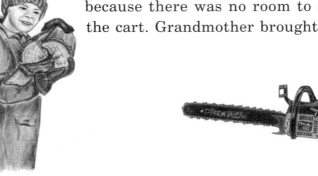

steaming hot chocolate out for the workers. Mother carried some freshly baked cinnamon rolls.

"The children loaded the cart," Father said, smiling as he took a bite of his cinnamon roll. He looked at Galen and Mabel. "After we have unloaded and stacked this load, you do not need to help anymore."

When the wood was unloaded, Father and Grandfather left for the big tree again.

Galen and Mabel did not know what to do. So Galen suggested, "Let's go the second mile for Grandfather."

"The second mile?" Mabel did not understand.

"Yes. Remember when Father explained in family devotions that if we do more work than we have to, it is like going the second mile? The first mile is

what we are *asked* to do, but the second mile is the extra that we *choose* to do."

"Do you mean you want to load more wood for Grandfather?" Mabel asked.

"Yes, I would like to help Grandfather with another load of wood, even though Father said we do not have to do it," Galen explained. "Do you want to go with me to the big tree again?"

"Yes, I want to help some more too," Mabel agreed. "I will ask Mother if it is all right for us to go."

As they walked out the long lane, Galen said, "Father also told us that usually the extra work that we do is easier and more interesting because we *choose* to do it."

When Galen and Mabel arrived at the big tree, they smiled at Father.

"We decided to go the second mile," Galen explained with a hearty laugh.

"We want to help with another load," Mabel explained.

Father smiled too. He knew what Galen meant about the second mile. He  knew that the children wanted to help Grandfather with another load. "I am sure you will be happy for doing more than you had to," Father said. Then he picked up his chain saw and started sawing again.

Grandfather was pleased when Galen told him they would help with another load. "God bless you, my dear children!" he said.

By dinnertime, the cart was again piled full of wood and two extra-happy and extra-hungry children ate Grandmother's macaroni-and-cheese dinner.

2.

The Missing Worksheet

Phoebe opened the car door. "Hello, Mother!" she sang out cheerily.

"Good afternoon," Mother returned as she carefully drove the van away from school.

"I am on my way home from town, so you may help me put the groceries away after we get home," Mother said as they turned onto the highway.

When they got home, Phoebe was excited about helping Mother. But first she emptied her lunch box and put

her arithmetic worksheet on the desk. "Mother, Sister Elaine sent this worksheet home with me. I need to finish it tonight."

"All right," Mother agreed. "You will have time to do it after supper."

Then Phoebe began putting away the groceries. She knew where Mother wanted her to put most of the things. "Mother, where do you want me to put these light bulbs?"

"They go in the upstairs bathroom," Mother told her.

Phoebe hurried up the stairs, singing as she went. She stacked the light bulbs in the closet.

Soon all the groceries were put away, and Phoebe went to play with her brother on the swing.

After supper, Mother reminded Phoebe, "You should do your

Arithmetic   *Phoebe*
Worksheet 3
Part 1 Addition
(1.) 23   (2.) 64   (3.) 45   (4.) 8
   + 19   + 51   + 10   + 99

(5.) 120 (6.) 230 (7.) 377 (8.) 408
   + 54   + 83   + 103   + 222

Part 2 Subtraction
(1.) 32   (2.) 79   (3.) 96   (4.) 112
   − 8   − 72   − 78   − 40

arithmetic worksheet now."

Phoebe walked to the desk. "Where is my paper?" she thought. "I know I put it on this desk."

Phoebe searched for the missing paper. She searched through a stack of papers. She searched under the books. She searched on the floor around the desk. "The paper is not here," Phoebe thought sadly. "Sister Elaine will not be happy."

Phoebe looked around some more. She looked for her paper for five min-

utes. "Mother!" she called. Then she quickly added, "Nothing after all!"

Quickly Phoebe hurried up the steps. She went to pray about her paper. "Dear Lord," she prayed, "I cannot find my arithmetic paper. Please help me to find it. Thank You. In Jesus' Name. Amen."

Phoebe jumped up and walked slowly down the stairs to the desk again.

She was thinking and thinking. Then suddenly she saw a paper sticking out between two books. "That looks like my worksheet," she said excitedly. And it was!

"Thank You, Lord, for helping me to find it!" Phoebe exclaimed. Happily Phoebe went and told Mother her story.

The next day at school, Phoebe also told Sister Elaine about the lost paper.

"I am glad that God helped you to find it," Sister Elaine rejoiced. "Sometimes God chooses not to answer our prayers that quickly, but this time it was His will to help you right away. You must remember to thank Him."

"I did thank Him," Phoebe said quietly. "God cared about my paper."

"Yes, He really did," Sister Elaine agreed.

Arithmetic   Phoebe

Worksheet 3

Part 1 Addition

(1.) 23 (2.) 64 (3.) 45 (4.) 8
$+19$ $+51$ $+10$ $+99$

(5.) 120 (6.) 230 (7.) 377 (8.) 408
$+54$ $+83$ $+102$ $+222$

Part 2 Subtraction

(1.) 32 (2.) 79 (3.) 96 (4.) 112
-8 -72 -78 -40

3.

Caught on the
Fishing Line

Anna slid her lunch box onto the kitchen counter. "Mother," she announced, "Sister Ellen is making a fishing line at school." She chuckled.

"A what?" Mother stopped her sewing and looked at Anna.

"A fishing line," Anna repeated, grinning. "Sister Ellen says that we forget to do too many things. From now on, if we forget something, a fish with our

name will be hung on the fishing line. Each fish has a hook in its mouth, ready to be hung on the fishing line. We must remember things; then our fish won't get hung up there."

"That is a good idea," Mother said. "You must remember the things that you are supposed to do. You will make Sister Ellen's job a lot easier if you do not need to be reminded."

"I know," Anna said. She took a bite out of her cookie. "If we forget two times in a week, we will need to do a lot of writing to help us remember things better," she added.

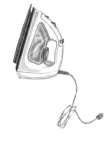

"I think that would help," Mother agreed.

A week later Anna brought a paper home from school.

"What are you doing with that paper?" Mother asked.

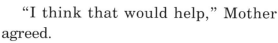

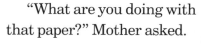

"Oh, I forgot to write my name on my paper twice this week," Anna said. "Now I must do some writing."

Mother frowned as she looked at the paper. Across the top Sister Ellen had neatly written, "Write this thirty times: I will remember to put my name on my paper."

Then Mother spoke kindly. "You were careless to forget to write your name on your paper. You should check your paper every time to make sure you put your name on it."

Anna nodded slowly. "I didn't think about checking over my paper."

Anna started writing her sentence. A while later she sighed. "Mother, my fingers are sore. I am tired of writing. May I finish this later tonight?" she asked.

"Oh, no!" Mother answered.

"The Bible says that we must reap what we sow. You were careless this week; now you must suffer for it."

Anna had tears in her eyes as she continued writing. She really was tired, but she knew it was her fault.

After quite a while, Anna let out a big sigh. Mother looked up from her ironing.

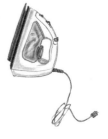

"I am finished, Mother!" Anna could smile again. "I am going to try really hard to remember to write my name on my papers."

Mother smiled. "I am glad. That will make Sister Ellen happy too. Don't get caught on the fishing line next week!"

"I will try not to get caught," Anna said, laughing, as she put her paper in her book bag.

4.

Marcus Builds Too

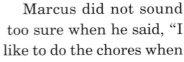

"Marcus," began Father one morning at the breakfast table, "I need to help build the new church house again today. I want you to do the chicken chores as we usually do them."

Marcus slowly cut his egg. He looked at Father. Father smiled back at him.

"You want to do that, don't you?"

Marcus did not sound too sure when he said, "I like to do the chores when

you help me, but it takes so long when I do them all by myself."

"I understand," Father agreed. "It does take much longer when you do them alone. But this summer I am help-ing to build the new church house, so I do not have as much time to help you."

"I wish that I were old enough to help build the church house too." Marcus looked eagerly at Father.

Father chuckled, but then his face became sober. "You know, Marcus, you really are helping to build our new church house."

Marcus did not understand. "How am I doing that?"

Father put jelly on a slice of toast for Rose Ann, and then he answered, "Because you do the chores for me, I am able to go to work earlier in the

morning. If I needed to do the chores, I would not be ready to go for another half an hour. If I work an extra half hour every morning that you do the chores for me, I will work many more hours."

"But that is helping in a different way than I thought," Marcus said. Then he took the last bite of his toast.

Mother smiled. "Yes, it is helping in a different way, but it helps a lot. I cannot build a church house either; but every time the food committee asks me to cook food for the men who work there, then I am helping to build too."

"That is right, Mother." Father smiled at Mother. "The Bible says, 'We are labourers together with God.' That means we help each other and we help God."

"Do I help build too?" Rose Ann asked seriously.

"Yes, Rose Ann. When you help Mother dry the dishes when she cooks for the men who are working, then you are helping to build the church house too," Father said.

Then the whole family had to laugh because suddenly everyone was helping to build the new church house.

Marcus said, "I will feed the chickens, Father. Maybe someday I can truly help to build a church house."

"Maybe you can," Father agreed.

5.

Matthew's Dollar Bill

Mother and Matthew were on their way to town. "We will stop to visit Mrs. Zang," Mother explained as they drove along.

"I am glad," Matthew said. Mrs. Zang used to be their neighbor, but now she lived in town. So they did not see her very often.

Mother pulled off the busy highway into Mrs. Zang's driveway.

"Come in! Come in!" Mrs. Zang invited them eagerly. She was indeed

happy to see them.

Matthew gave her the loaf of home-made bread that Mother had brought along. Mrs. Zang exclaimed, "Oh, thank you so much. I love homemade bread!"

When Mother and Matthew were getting ready to leave, Mrs. Zang hurried off to her bedroom. Soon she was back. "I want to give this to you," she said, handing Matthew a dollar bill. "I want you to buy something that you like."

Now it was Matthew's turn to be surprised. "Thank you!" he managed to say as he looked at Mother.

"You are welcome," Mrs. Zang replied. "I like when you come with your mother to see me. Come again!"

As they drove to the store, Matthew said, "Mother, I would like to buy something for David, to surprise him.

What does David need?"

"Well," Mother said thoughtfully, "if you are sure you want to spend the money for David, then why don't you help me choose some material to make a Sunday shirt. Then I will sew a shirt for him, and you can give the shirt to him."

"Yes, I like that idea." Matthew was excited. "Let's keep it a secret until you have the shirt made. Okay, Mother?"

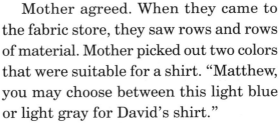

Mother agreed. When they came to the fabric store, they saw rows and rows of material. Mother picked out two colors that were suitable for a shirt. "Matthew, you may choose between this light blue or light gray for David's shirt."

Matthew thought and thought. Finally he said, "Mother, I like the light gray the best. Do I have enough money for it?"

"Yes, you do," Mother answered. "We like this light gray material," she told the saleslady.

The lady cut the material and put it in a bag. Then after paying for the material, Mother and Matthew left the store.

Mother soon made David's shirt, so Matthew did not have to wait long to give David his gift.

"The shirt for David is finished," Mother told Matthew one evening. "Would you like to give it to him tonight?"

"Oh, yes, I would." Matthew left his toys on the floor. "Where is it?"

"Come with me." Mother went to the sewing room closet. "I put it on a hanger for you."

"David!" Matthew called. "Come here!"

David came to the sewing

room. "I bought this for you." Matthew gave the new shirt to David.

David was surprised; then Mother and Matthew explained about Matthew's dollar bill.

Finally David remembered to say, "Thank you, Matthew, for buying it. And thank you, Mother, for making my shirt."

"You are welcome," they said together.

Then Mother went back to the closet. "Matthew, I have a gift for you too," she said with a smile.

Matthew's eyes opened wide when Mother gave him a light gray shirt for Sunday. It matched David's. "Oh, Mother, did you make one for me too?" he exclaimed.

Mother smiled. "Yes, I wanted to make one for you too because you were willing to spend your dollar bill for David."

"Thank you, Mother. I didn't know you made one for me."

"You are welcome," Mother said. "God loves a cheerful giver, so I decided to be a cheerful giver too."

6.

A Good Patient

Dorcas sighed loudly as she pulled the covers up to her chin again. This was the third day she was sick. "Mother, I am so tired of lying here all the time. I want my sore throat to go away. I want to go to school again."

"I know, Dorcas," Mother said as she sat on the couch beside Dorcas. "We are asking God to heal you. But sometimes we must be patient and wait until our bodies heal. Shall I tell you a story about John?"

Dorcas swallowed painfully but nodded her head.

Mother started. "When John was born, he was not a healthy baby like you were. After he grew up to be a man, he could no longer keep his balance while walking. Whenever we saw John, he was in a wheelchair."

Mother smiled sadly as she remembered John. Then she continued, "John needed to spend the rest of his life in a special hospital. He was not well. But the doctors and nurses enjoyed taking care of him. Can you guess why?"

"Was he happy?" Dorcas guessed.

Mother smiled. "You are right. John was a very good patient. Whenever a person walked past his wheelchair, John would say, 'Hello. Have a happy day.'

"Do you think you can be like John? You are getting better. Soon you may go

back to school again."

Dorcas grinned a little. "I can try," she said. "Have a happy day, Mother!"

"Same to you, Dorcas," Mother replied, laughing.

As Dorcas rested on the couch that afternoon, she thought about John. "I am glad that I do not need a wheelchair," she whispered to herself.

When Father came into the house for supper, Dorcas peeked out from under her covers. "Have a happy day, Father!"

Father looked surprised. So Dorcas told him about John. "I decided to be like John so that I could be happy," she finished.

"I am glad," Father said as he sat on his chair. "God cares for us. No matter what happens to us, He is still our heavenly Father."

7.

Grandmother's Helper

"David!" Mother called. "Grand-mother just called. She needs your help to do her grocery shopping. Would you like to go to town with her?"

David came running. "Yes. I love help-ing Grandmother," he said eagerly.

"I know you do, David. I am glad that you help Grandmother will-ingly. The Bible tells us to care for the widows. Father and I are trying to do that by caring for

Grandmother."

David changed into clean clothes and neatly combed his hair. He waited patiently until he saw Grandmother's car come in the driveway.

"Good-bye, Mother," he called.

"Good-bye," Mother said, waving at him.

"I am so glad that you can go with me," Grandmother said as she turned the car around. "It is hard for me to reach some things, and it's especially hard to empty my cart of groceries."

"I am glad that you want me to go with you, Grandmother. I like to help you."

Grandmother did not shop in the grocery store very often, so she needed lots of things. David carefully pushed the cart for Grandmother. She crossed things off her list as they found

them. "David, I need this bag of potatoes. Would you please lift it into the cart
for me?"

David carefully placed the potatoes in
the cart beside the bag of flour they had
gotten. "Now I need a head of lettuce."
David chose a big head of lettuce and car-
ried it to the cart.

David helped Grandmother find many
other things. Finally Grandmother had
marked everything off her long list.
"We will pay over there." Grandmother
pointed to the checkout counter that had
a number 3 on top of it.

Without being told what to do, David
carefully put the groceries on the counter for the lady to scan the prices. "You
have a good helper." The clerk smiled at
Grandmother as Grandmother prepared
to write her check.

"Yes, I do," Grandmother agreed. "He

is my grandson, and his help made every-thing so much easier for me today."

"I can see that!" the clerk agreed.

When they arrived at Grandmother's house, David carried all the bags into the house. He put them on the table as Grandmother asked him to do. Then he helped put the heavy things where Grandmother wanted them.

Grandmother sat on her chair and sighed. "That was a big job. Thank you so much for your help."

"You are welcome," David replied.

After they had a drink and ate some watermelon, Grandmother took David home. She visited with Mother and thanked her for allowing David to go with her. Then she left.

"Did you have a nice time?" Mother asked David.

"Yes, Mother, I did," David

said, nodding his head.

"I am so glad you did it cheerfully, son," said Mother.

8.

Time to Obey

One afternoon, nine-year-old Anna and her younger sister Carol were playing school in their bedroom. Suddenly Carol looked at the alarm clock. "Anna!" she exclaimed. "It is four o'clock. We must go. Mother wants us to get the wood inside at four o'clock."

"Oh," sighed Anna, "it will be light outside for a while yet. I want to finish your arithmetic class first."

"Okay," Carol agreed. "Then we must

go right away."

But after arithmetic class was over, Anna remembered the story she wanted to read to Carol. "Story time," she announced with a smile. "This won't take long. It is only five minutes after four," she stated, noticing Carol's frown.

Five minutes passed. Ten minutes went by. Carol was enjoying the stories, so Anna kept on reading.

A while later, Mother called from the kitchen, "Girls, please come and set the table for me. Father will be in for supper before long."

Anna gasped. "Carol!" she exclaimed. Alarm rang in her voice.

"What time is it, Anna?" Carol managed to whisper.

"It is four-thirty," Anna answered after checking the alarm clock. Quietly the girls walked to the

kitchen. Quickly they set the table.

"Mother, we didn't bring the wood in yet. May we hurry and do it before Father comes in?" Anna finally asked.

Mother was stirring the gravy. "No," she answered, looking at the girls soberly. "You do not have enough time to bring it in before supper. You must get it in later. I am sorry that you disobeyed me and did not watch the clock as we had planned."

"Oh, Mother," Carol sighed. "After supper it will be dark and cold outside."

"I know, Carol," Mother agreed. "But you did not do your work on time. Now you will need to do it anyway, even if it is not as easy to do it after supper. Come with me to the study. You girls need to be punished."

After the dishes were washed and dried, two sober girls dressed in their coats, boots, scarves, and warm mittens.

They stepped outside into the cold winter night and hurried to the woodpile. The snow was blowing, and the wind made their faces cold. They carried load after load of wood into the house.

Thirty minutes later, Anna arranged the last piece of wood on the neat stack beside the wood stove. "I'm going to try to remember to always obey Mother," she declared as she warmed her hands by the wood stove.

"I am too," Carol determined.

9.

Rachel Helps Her Sister

"Good-bye," Mother said and smiled at seven-year-old Rachel. As Father and Mother drove out the driveway, Rachel returned their waves and then turned to her big sister, Beth.

"Shall I wash the breakfast dishes for you?" she asked.

"Yes, that would be nice," Beth replied. "I am so glad that you are going to help me today. We have a lot of work to do. Mother was sorry

that she had to leave, but her tooth hurt her so much that she needed to see a special doctor to pull it out."

Rachel washed the dishes while Beth mixed a batch of bread. Before long they were both finished. Beth said, "Please get four buckets from the garage, Rachel. We need to pick the tomatoes."

"Good," Rachel said, and she ran for the buckets. Together they went to the garden. Beth filled her second bucket just as Rachel filled her first one. "I am so glad for your help." Beth smiled. "We are getting a good start on the work for today."

Beth's words made Rachel feel happy inside. Soon four buckets of red tomatoes stood beside the sink in the kitchen. "Would you like to wash the tomatoes for me?" Beth asked. "I will cut them into pieces."

"Sure," Rachel said with a smile. She

worked quickly because Beth could cut tomatoes really fast. "I do not want you to wait on me." Rachel laughed, dropping another tomato into the clean bowl.

Splash, wash, drop, *splash*, wash, drop. Many tomatoes went through Rachel's busy hands. After the tomatoes were finished cooking, Rachel turned the strainer handle for Beth. The tomatoes were hot, so Rachel had to be careful lest she burn herself.

Beth filled the clean jars with the tomato juice. "You may put a teaspoon of salt in each jar, Rachel," Beth instructed. "Then I will close the jars, and we will set them on the floor. Mother will process them when she gets home."

Father and Mother returned about that time. Mother was surprised. "Are you almost finished with the tomatoes?" she asked. "Thank you,

girls!" Mother smiled.

Beth smiled. "Almost! Rachel helped me so much. I would not have been able to do this much alone."

"Oh, you are welcome," Rachel replied. "It was fun being Beth's helper."

10.

No More Stars

Mark was the only one in first grade. He liked to go to school. He especially enjoyed learning how to read. When Sister Ruth called his class to read, Mark picked up his reading book and went to the class table.

"Sister Ruth, I can read all the stories from here to here." Mark showed his teacher his book. "I studied them at home last evening."

"Good for you!" Sister Ruth smiled.

100% ★

"You are learning more every day."

Mark read his reading story for Sister Ruth. Then he went back to his desk and filled in the blanks in his workbook. He read the questions carefully so that he could get all the answers correct. He wanted to get a star at the top of his page.

Each day Mark read the whole story to Sister Ruth because there were no other first graders. But one day something changed.

James, who was in the second grade, was Mark's friend. They played together before school in the morning. James often had homework. He was not at the same place in his books as the other second graders were.

One morning when Mark came to school, James had different books lying on his desk. He had books like Mark's. He would be in first grade now.

When it was time for first-grade read-ing class, two boys went to the class table. When it was time to read the story, two boys read the story to Sister Ruth.

It was not long before Mark noticed something. "James finishes his work long before I do," he thought. "I will hurry today."

That day when Mark got his work-book back from his teacher, he had no star at the top of the page. He had ten answers wrong, and Sister Ruth asked him to correct the wrong ones.

The next day Mark had no star on his work either. For five days Mark had no star in his reading workbook.

Then one evening Mark saw Sister Ruth talking to Mother for quite a while.

That evening Father and Mother talked to Mark.

"Son, Sister Ruth tells us

that since James is in your class, you hurry with your work, and you have not gotten any stars on your pages. Why do you hurry so much?" Father asked kindly.

Mark looked at Father. At first, he did not know what to say. Then he said, "James finishes so long before I do."

Father understood. "Mark, James went to school last year too, and he learned how to read then. He can read faster than you can because he has been reading much longer than you have. You must read more slowly so that you can answer the questions correctly. First grade will be easy for James for a while, but he needs to review it so that he can do second-grade work better next year."

"Sister Ruth wants you to do good work like you were doing before James was in your grade," Mother said. "She knows

that you can get stars on your work."

"Do your best," Father encouraged Mark. "Whatever we do, we are doing it for the Lord. That means we want to be sure we are doing it right."

"Yes, Father," Mark replied.

The next day when the boys had finished reading their story to Sister Ruth, she looked at Mark and said, "Boys, do your lesson neatly and carefully."

Mark flashed her a smile. He knew she was talking to him, and he was going to do his best.

Before long Mark glanced over at James. "Oh," he sighed. "James is done with the first page already." He wanted to hurry, but he remembered Father's words.

Pretty soon Mark heard James close his book. Sadly Mark watched James put his book on Sister Ruth's desk. Then

Mark saw Sister Ruth watching him.

"Mark," she encouraged him, "take your time to do it right."

Mark had a whole page of work to do yet, but he kept on being careful. He wanted to be able to tell Father and Mother that he had gotten a star on his page that day.

Sister Ruth checked his book after he was finished. "Mark, you got every answer correct," she said with a smile.

Father and Mother were happy when Mark told them that he had gotten a star in his reading workbook that day.

Sometimes after that, Mark forgot to do his best. It was hard to go slowly when James was already finished with his workbook. But he wanted to do his work correctly and please Sister Ruth. He knew that was the right thing to do. And he wanted to get a star too.

11.

The Peach Decision

"Mother, Grandpa is here!" Jerald called from the porch swing, where he had been watching for the black Chevy truck.

"Good-bye, Jerald," Mother called from the screen door. "I hope you have a good time with Grandpa. Hurry back."

Jerald had just enough time to give Mother a big smile before jumping into Grandpa's old farm truck.

"Grandpa, help yourself to some

peaches from the trees on your way out the lane," Mother called from the porch.

Grandpa waved in reply. He backed the truck around and headed out the lane.

"It's a beautiful morning, isn't it, Jerald?" Grandpa smiled.

"Yes," Jerald agreed. He enjoyed going with Grandpa to town. When Grandpa stopped the truck to get some peaches, Jerald said excitedly, "Grandpa, the peaches from this tree are extra good. Father says so." Jerald pointed toward the tree that was loaded with fruit.

"Really?" Grandpa walked to that tree. He reached up and got a peach for Jerald and one for

himself. Grandpa took a bite. "You are right, Jerald," he agreed. "This peach *is* very good."

Jerald held his peach in his hand and turned it round and round. It looked really good, and it felt juicy. But he would wait to eat it until they were on their way to town.

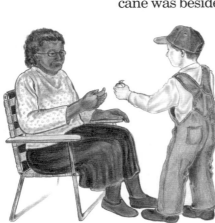

Grandpa and Jerald got back into the old Chevy truck. Jerald snapped his seat belt into place, and they headed down the road. Soon Grandpa slowed down again. "I need to get the mail at the post office before we go to town," he told Jerald as he stopped at the green building.

Jerald noticed Mrs. Campbell sitting on her porch next to the post office. Her cane was beside her chair. He waved to her, and she waved back. Sometimes Grandma would visit Mrs. Campbell. One time last year the schoolchildren had come to sing songs for her. "She liked that!" Jerald remembered.

Suddenly Jerald noticed that he still had his peach in his hand. "I could give my peach to Mrs. Campbell," he thought, still watching Mrs. Campbell on her porch. "But I wanted to eat it. It looks so good." Jerald rolled the peach around in his hand several times. Then he thought of something.

Click! went his seat belt. He opened the truck door and walked the few steps to Mrs. Campbell's porch. "Mrs. Campbell, you may have this peach," Jerald offered kindly.

"Oh, thank you!" Mrs. Campbell's face beamed. "Did your father grow this?"

Jerald nodded. "Yes. Father has peach trees in the orchard."

"That is nice," she

replied. "Thank you. Thank you."

"You are welcome." Jerald hurried back to the truck.

When Grandpa came out of the post office, Jerald said, "Grandpa, I gave my peach to Mrs. Campbell."

"That was a nice thing to do," Grandpa said as he smiled and waved to Mrs. Campbell, who was sitting on her porch, enjoying her fresh peach.

"I really wanted to keep it," Jerald admitted. "But then I thought of it that Jesus would share with her. I can eat another one when we get home from town."

"It makes us happy to share, doesn't it?" Grandpa smiled.

"Yes," Jerald agreed. "I know that Mrs. Campbell was happy, and Mother says we should be kind to the widows."

Recess Time for Eric

Third-grader Eric glanced up from his math book. He looked at the clock on the wall. "It is almost recess time," he thought. "I hope we play prisoner's base again today." Then he wrote another answer on his paper.

"Recess time," Sister Sarah announced. "We will play prisoner's base. I think we will keep the same teams today that we had yesterday."

Eric almost clapped his hands. He was

so excited.

Yesterday he had gotten caught only once all recess. "Maybe I won't get caught at all today," he thought, smiling to himself.

As the boys were walking to the playground, they were making big plans. "Let's guard our base extra well today," Eric instructed his teammates.

"Yes," Daniel agreed. "Yesterday I was so happy when we put Phyllis into prison. She runs like a deer!"

"I know," Jerald sighed. "I stay away from her too."

"Everyone ready?" Sister Sarah asked. "The game is on!"

What fun Eric had! He pretended that he was not scared of the other team. Of course, when someone left the base after he did, he ran back to his base quickly.

Eric forgot about Phyllis for a little

while. Suddenly from behind him she was coming very fast. Eric darted for the base, but he was too late.

"Caught!" Phyllis said as she tagged him.

"I was almost on base." Eric glared at Phyllis. "You think you can run so fast!"

"I do not," Phyllis said as she returned to her base. She was happy that she had caught a prisoner.

"You do too!" Eric started walking toward the prison.

Sister Sarah walked to Eric. She looked into his angry eyes. "Eric, you must go in and take your seat. You may not play anymore this recess. There is no reason for you to be so angry at Phyllis. Work on your math until I come in."

Eric was sad. He had been angry, but he did want to play some more. Recess had just begun.

Eric took a drink at the fountain. Then he started on his math lesson. While he worked, he heard happy voices outside. He knew it was his own fault that he was inside.

When Sister Sarah came in, she looked kindly at Eric. "Your parents and I want you to be kind to each other, as the Bible teaches. If you are angry at the other children, you are not being kind to them. Will you try to do better, Eric?"

"Yes," he said.

When Sister Sarah announced the next recess, she said, "We will play 'kick the stick' today."

"Oh, no. Phyllis is it," Eric groaned to Daniel.

"Let's keep away from her," Jerald warned.

Eric thought that he would stay away from Phyllis, but Phyllis was determined that all the third-grade boys would get caught before someone kicked the stick. She chased Eric and touched his arm.

"Caught!"

Eric turned around. Suddenly he felt angry again. "You—" he started to say. Then he quickly remembered that he did not want to lose another recess. So he turned to accept being caught.

He looked at Sister Sarah. She had noticed. She smiled when Eric looked at her. He had done better.

13.

Playtime Troubles

"I like to play foursquare, don't you?" Mae asked Lori excitedly as she placed her lunch box on the shelf. She took her place at the end of the line of children waiting their turn at the game.

"Yes, I do!" Lori agreed, stepping in line behind Mae.

"I do not like when John gets us out though." Mae sighed, wishing John would not be the server.

"Good!" A chorus of cheers sounded

as John missed the ball a bit later. He took his place at the end of the line, and Mary entered the fourth square. Now Marcus moved up to the serving position.

"Marcus is out!"

"No! No!" Marcus raised his voice to be heard above the others. "It hit the line. The ball hit the line!"

"Did it?"

"Do it over." One rule in this game was that if the children were not sure who was out, they were allowed to do it over.

Everyone agreed except Mae. She slipped out of the line. She met Sister Anna in the hallway with the bell in her hand.

"Sister Anna, Marcus did not take his out," she stated.

"Did the others say he was out too?" Sister Anna asked quietly.

"They did it over," Mae replied.

"That is the rule, isn't it?" Sister Anna asked kindly.

Mae nodded and slipped to her desk as the bell rang.

The next day at recess, Mae went to the teacher again. "Sister Anna, Rosanna and Lori do not want me on their base today."

"I need someone on my base," Sister Anna answered.

Then Mae said, "I asked to be with Lori before Rosanna did."

"Stay with me now," Sister Anna told her.

The next day Mae tattled again. "Sister Anna, James pushed Mark when they were in line."

"Mae," Sister Anna said quietly. "Go to the classroom. I want to talk to you."

Mae hung her head. She walked slowly

to her desk.

A little later Sister Anna came to the classroom. "Mae," she began, "who is the teacher in this classroom?"

Mae looked surprised. "You are, Sister Anna."

"That is right," Sister Anna agreed. "God wants me to be a good teacher. You must let me tell the other children what to do. If someone does something wrong and I am not there, you must tell me. But if it is something small and I am nearby, you should not tattle about everything. You keep right on playing. Then if someone misbehaves, I will try to notice it. Do you understand?"

Mae nodded her head. She understood, because Mother had told her not to tattle on the others at home.

Mae looked at Sister Anna. "I will

try not to tattle anymore."

Sister Anna smiled. "That is good. The Bible says that we are to obey them who have the rule over us. You may go now."

A few days later, the children were playing foursquare a few minutes before school started. It was the favorite game for the children at Mt. Zion School.

"You are out, Marcus," everyone agreed. Marcus took the ball and bounced it really high. It hit the ceiling.

"Oh," thought Mae. "It almost hit the light. I will tell Sister Anna." Suddenly she stopped. "No, I will not. It did not hit the light, and I do not want to be a tattletale."

The game went on, and everyone was happy. Mae was the happiest because she had remembered to obey Sister Anna.

14.

A Letter
for Grandmother

Seven-year-old Elsie stretched as
she stood up from where she had been
reading on the couch. She had just finished her new book, *Gone to the Zoo*.
"I like Carol in this book," she thought
as she placed the book carefully in the
bookcase.

"Mother, what are you doing?" Elsie
asked as she entered the office, where
Mother was sitting at her desk.

"I am writing a letter to Grandmother," Mother answered as she kept on writing.

"I wish that I could write letters," Elsie sighed. "I would like to do that."

"Well, why don't you write a letter to Grandmother," Mother suggested. "We can fold it and send it to Grandmother in my envelope."

"I would like to do that," Elsie said eagerly, "but I never wrote a letter before. Do you think that I could do it, Mother?" Her brown eyes looked soberly into Mother's face.

"Yes, I think you can." Mother smiled at Elsie. "Go find a pencil in the drawer. Then I will give you some paper to write your letter on."

Elsie hurried to the drawer and got her pencil. Mother found a pretty piece of stationery that had apples on it.

"Grandmother likes apples, so I will give you this paper with apples on it," Mother said.

"Thank you!" Elsie beamed. "What shall I write to Grandmother?"

"You could tell her about all the corn we put in the freezer last week," Mother suggested. "Grandmother likes to hear about our animals too."

"Will you help me if I cannot spell some words?" Elsie asked.

"I surely will," Mother agreed.

Elsie sat at the kitchen table. She thought about Grandmother, who lived far away. Then she began writing.

Dear Grandmother Schrock,

I love you. I pray for you when I go to bed. I help Mother with the dishes. We got a lot of corn from the garden. I helped take off the . . .

"Mother, how do you spell *husks*?"

"H-u-s-k-s," Mother spelled slowly.

"Thank you." Elsie smiled as she continued her letter.

> . . . *husks off the corn. David helped too. I can hardly wait for school to start. I will be in second grade. It is warm here. We have two cats. I hope you are well. Please come see us soon.*
>
> *Love, Elsie*

"That looks good." Mother was pleased when she read Elsie's letter. "Grandmother is a widow, since Grandfather died, and the Bible tells us that we should visit the widows. Writing a letter is another way to visit Grandmother. I know Grandmother will be pleased with your letter."

"I am glad," Elsie said happily.

A few days later, Grandmother opened

Mother's letter. Then she found Elsie's letter. "Thank you, God, for Elsie's letter. Bless my granddaughter who lives far away," Grandmother prayed. She was so happy for Elsie's letter.

15.

Keeping On and On

Matthew was in first grade. When someone gave out the number of a song in school devotions, Matthew quickly found it in his songbook. He liked to sing; but more than that, he liked to find the page numbers all by himself.

One day Brother Joseph was having devotions for the children. "I would like to sing number 74," Brother Joseph announced. "I want to speak about perseverance this morning. Do you know

what that means?"

Matthew smiled at Sister Judith; but he did not raise his hand, because he was not sure.

"Let's sing the song," said Brother Joseph. "Then I will tell you what it means."

"'When a weary task you find it, / Persevere and never mind it; / Never mind it, never mind it,'" the children sang.

Then Brother Joseph explained. "*Perseverance* means keeping on and on—even when your lesson is a long lesson." He told the story of two boys. One boy persevered, and the other boy gave up easily. "God will help you persevere in your schoolwork," Brother Joseph finished.

"I want to be like Richard in that story," Matthew decided. "He kept right on working even though his fingers were

cold. He grew up to be a good man."

A few days later, Sister Judith gave each of the first graders a sheet of paper. It had many spaces that were empty. She smiled at Justin and Matthew. "Do you remember what Brother Joseph said in devotions on Monday morning about perseverance?"

Matthew nodded his head eagerly. He remembered Brother Joseph's story about Richard.

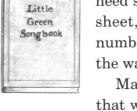

Sister Judith's face was serious, but her eyes were smiling. "Today you will need some perseverance. On this worksheet, you will need to start with the number one and write the numbers all the way to five hundred."

Matthew looked at his sheet. "Oh, that will take a long time," he thought. But he smiled at Sister Judith and got out a sharp pencil.

"It will take you a long time, but you can do it," she encouraged them. "You know your numbers quite well. You may begin now."

Matthew started writing. He made each number neatly. "It is easy," he thought as he wrote *32, 33, 34, . . .*

Finally he reached the number 100. He was glad, but he also saw the many spaces that needed to be filled yet.

Soon Sister Judith announced, "Recess time!"

Little Green Songbook

Matthew sighed with relief. "Sister Judith," he said when they were dismissed, "I just finished number 169."

"Good for you!" Sister Judith smiled. "You are doing quite well."

"Sister Judith, I am at number 156," Justin said.

"Good," Sister Judith said, smiling at him. "That is very good too. You have

been busy boys."

After recess, Matthew worked on his paper again. "I will try to get a lot done before reading class." He wrote *170, 171, 172.* His head was bent over his paper as he worked diligently. He was persevering.

After finishing his reading lesson, Matthew wrote numbers again. He worked for a long time. "Oh-h-h," he sighed. His pencil was dull now, and his fingers were sore. Sister Judith heard his sigh, and Matthew raised his hand.

"I am at four hundred now," he said.

"Very good," Sister Judith praised him. "Only one hundred more to go."

Matthew picked up a sharp pencil. He was tired of doing numbers. Justin told Sister Judith that he was almost finished. But then Matthew remembered Richard in Brother Joseph's story. "I want to be like Richard," he told himself again.

And then it did not seem long until Matthew raised his hand eagerly. "I am finished!" he announced happily. His eyes were shining.

"Very good, Matthew!" Sister Judith exclaimed. "Do you remember what *perseverance* means?"

Matthew nodded. "Keeping on and on until you are finished."

Sister Judith praised him. "That is just what you did."

Matthew was happy. He had finished his long lesson.

16.

A Surprise
for Sister Faith

"Did your mother tell you about the surprise Sister Julie is planning for Sister Faith?" Irma quietly asked her friend Katie on Monday morning before they entered their classroom.

"Yes, she did," Katie answered. "I am so excited about it!"

Irma smiled eagerly. "I am too! But we must be very quiet about it, or we will spoil the surprise."

"I know," Katie agreed. "That is what my mother said too."

All the first, second, and third graders knew about the surprise for Sister Faith. They were eager for Friday, the last day of school, to come. That was when they would give the surprise scrapbook to Sister Faith.

That evening at home, Irma wiped the dishes quickly. "Mother said she will help me do my scrapbook sheet tonight," Irma told her big sister Marie. "That is why I am in a hurry with the dishes."

Marie gave Irma a big smile. "I am glad that you can make a surprise for Sister Faith."

After the dishes were finished, Mother found her box of scrapbook supplies. Irma slowly paged through the pictures. "Mother, here is a pretty sunset. May I glue it on the front of my scrapbook page?"

"That would be fine," Mother agreed. "Here, let me help you cut those edges just a little straighter." Mother picked up the scissors. "There now," she said as she finished. Mother paged through her poem book. "Here is a lovely poem about God painting the sky." Together Mother and Irma spread glue on the edges of the picture, and then Irma slowly printed the little poem on her sheet.

Mother came back to the table when Irma was finished writing the poem. "That is very nice," Mother commented. "It looks neat."

"I know this will make Sister Faith happy," Irma told Mother. "I would like to write something about school on the back side."

"I have an idea," Mother suggested. "On the top of the page, we will write,

'Remember When We . . .' Then I want you to think of the happy times you had this year. For each thing that you think about, we will cut out a little picture to go with it."

"I like that idea." Irma eagerly picked up an old magazine. "What shall the first one be?"

"Remember the hike you took last fall when the leaves were pretty? Right there is a picture of some woods," Mother said. "You cut around these lines I am making."

After Irma had cut around them, Mother said, "We will glue this square near the top of the page, and underneath it you may write '. . . took a hike.' Now your sentence reads, 'Remember when we took a hike.'"

Irma carefully did what Mother told her to do. "May I use these hot dogs to

remember our wiener roast?" she asked after paging through the magazine.

"Yes," Mother agreed.

It took a long time to fill the page. Irma remembered the hot lunches the mothers had brought, so she glued a picture of a steaming bowl of soup in one corner. She remembered the school trip to a doll factory, so she glued a picture of a doll on the page. Other things she remembered were singing together on Friday mornings, playing in the snow, making cards for Katie's sick grandfather, and working hard to get A's on a test.

At the bottom of the page, she wrote, "THANK YOU, SISTER FAITH."

"Now I am finished," Irma sighed after she had signed her name. She helped Mother clean off the table and throw all the scraps in the wastebasket.

"Mother," she said seriously, "I liked having Sister Faith for my teacher. This is a nice way of saying thank you to her."

"I think so too," Mother agreed.

On Friday morning, Sister Faith was surprised and pleased when Carol handed her a package with the scrapbook in it. "Thank you so much, children," she said after she had opened the package. "I will treasure this scrapbook. The Bible says, 'Even a child is known by his doings.' Each of you will be remembered by what you have done."

Irma was glad that Sister Faith was pleased.

17.

Violet Shares
Her Grandmother

"Grandmother is here! Grandmother is here!" Violet clapped her hands.

Mother opened the door; and with a smile, Grandmother Rose entered the living room. "Hello, children. I was to the store today, and I bought a surprise for you." She dug into her grocery bag and brought out a bag of oranges.

"Oh, oranges!" Violet held up the bag and smelled the oranges. "We have not

had oranges for a long time. Thank you, Grandmother."

"You are welcome," Grandmother said. "I must be going home to Grandfather now. I just wanted to give these oranges to you on my way home."

"Good-bye, Grandmother!" Violet waved to her from the window. "Come again sometime."

"Father, Grandmother was here today," Violet eagerly told Father as he washed his hands for supper. "She brought some oranges for us!"

"Really?" Father was pleased. The Berks family did not often buy oranges, so this was a special treat. At bedtime each one in the family was pleased to eat an orange from Grandmother.

Violet slowly ate a bite of an orange slice. Then she said, "Mother, Regina told me that she does not have any

Dear Regina,
My grandmother gives me lots of little treats. I want to share some of them with you because you do not have a grandmother. I love you for a friend.
Love,
Violet

grandmother, because both of her grand-mothers died when she was a baby. If Grandmother would not come, we would not have so much fun, because no one would give us treats like she does."

Mother nodded. "Yes. We would miss Grandmother very much if she died. I have an idea. You could share with Regina some of the things that Grand-mother gives to you. Then you would be sharing your grandmother with her."

"I would like that, Mother," Vio-let said as she tried to think of what she could give. "Shall I give one of my oranges?"

"Yes, that would be nice. Also, a while ago Grandmother gave you a new color-ing book, but I also have new ones in the drawer for you. Would you like to give Regina a coloring book?" Mother asked.

"Yes, I would," Violet agreed eagerly.

Mother and Violet put a coloring book and an orange in a gift bag. Then Violet wrote a note on some pretty paper.

> *Dear Regina,*
>
> *My grandmother gives me lots of little treats. I want to share some of them with you because you do not have a grandmother. I love you for a friend.*
>
> *Love, Violet*

Violet's heart was full of joy. She was doing something she knew would make Regina happy.

18.

Mrs. Palmer Forgets

The Reems family hurried home after the Sunday morning service. Six-year-old Rachel helped Mother set the table and dish out the hot food.

"I like to go to the nursing home," Rachel said with a smile after the prayer. "I like going up the elevators."

"I enjoy going to the nursing home too." Big brother Joseph smiled at Rachel. "But I think the most enjoyable part is singing for the elderly people after

we have had the elevator ride."

Rachel understood what Joseph meant. She nodded her head.

It was not long before the whole family was traveling to the nursing home. When they arrived, Rachel exclaimed, "I see Paul's, Nathan's, and Daniel's families!" Together the families walked to the tall building.

Soon the short elevator ride was over, and the families stood in front of the group of elderly people and sang song after song. Brother Daniel read a short Scripture and led in a prayer, after which they sang one more song.

Then Father, Mother, and Rachel walked around the room and shook hands with the elderly who had listened to them sing.

"Hello!" Mother smiled as she shook hands with Mrs. Palmer. "How are you

today?"

"Fine, thank you." Mrs. Palmer was happy for the visitors.

Then Mrs. Palmer turned to Rachel. "Hello," she said.

Rachel shook hands with Mrs. Palmer. "Hello," she said softly.

Mother and Mrs. Palmer visited some more. Soon Mrs. Palmer turned to Rachel again. "Hello," she said. She reached out to shake hands again.

Rachel quietly said "Hello" and shook Mrs. Palmer's hand.

"I don't know why she wanted to shake my hand again." Rachel was puzzled. "Maybe she thought I was another little girl."

Rachel had another surprise. Four more times before Father was ready to leave, Mrs. Palmer wanted to shake Rachel's hand. Each time she said "Hello"

all over again.

And each time Rachel shook Mrs. Palmer's hand politely and quietly said, "Hello." Mother smiled at Rachel, so Rachel knew she was doing the right thing, even though she did not understand it.

On the way home, Mother said to Rachel, "I was happy to see that you were kind and shook Mrs. Palmer's hand so often. She forgets things very easily. So each time that she saw you, she thought you had not shaken her hand before."

"I thought it was funny to shake the same person's hand six times!" Rachel exclaimed.

"But you didn't laugh at her, did you?" Father asked.

"Oh, no. I did not think she could help it," Rachel answered.

"She couldn't," Mother agreed. "You did the right thing by being kind."

19.

Norma's Candy Cup

"Happy birthday! Happy birthday!" Jason greeted his sister Norma as she entered the kitchen before breakfast.

"I know!" Norma laughed. "I thought about my birthday as soon as I opened my eyes this morning."

Mother set the sausage and pancakes on the table. "Come for breakfast, everyone," she called.

Soon breakfast and family devotions were over. Jason and Norma hurried to

get ready for school. "Good-bye," Father called as he waved to them. "Do your work well on your birthday, Norma."

"I will try," she promised.

Sister Elaine tapped her little bell. The pupils took their seats. "Good morning," Sister Elaine greeted them.

"Good morning," the children replied.

"Who can guess what our first song is this morning?" Sister Elaine smiled as if she knew a secret.

"'Happy Birthday.'" Second-grader Lois smiled at Norma.

"'Happy birthday to you! / Happy birthday to you! / Happy birthday, dear Norma, / Happy birthday to you!'" the class sang.

Norma smiled a thank-you to Sister Elaine and her friends. "Today is a happy day," Norma thought. "I like my birthday."

The day passed as a usual day, except

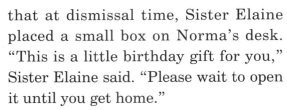

that at dismissal time, Sister Elaine placed a small box on Norma's desk. "This is a little birthday gift for you," Sister Elaine said. "Please wait to open it until you get home."

"Thank you!" Norma smiled.

"You are welcome," Sister Elaine replied.

Norma was very excited by the time she got home. She wondered so much what was in her box. Quickly she opened the little box. "A cup filled with Hershey Kisses!" Norma exclaimed. "See, my name and my birthday are on the cup too! See the cute kitten on this side?"

"That is a useful cup," Mother said with a smile. "You may put it on your dresser in your room."

Norma started for her room; then she looked back at Mother. "Are the Hershey Kisses all for me, or are they for everyone

in the family?" she asked.

Mother answered, "Sister Elaine gave the candy to you, so we will let you decide what you will do with it."

Norma walked slowly to her bedroom. She happened to glance back one time and saw her little brother Kevin and her sister Dorcas. They were watching her. Norma went to her room. "I want to make Dorcas and Kevin happy," she thought as she untied the ribbon and opened the plastic bag. She took out two Hershey Kisses. "I will share my birthday candy with them."

Norma walked out to the living room again. "Which hand do you want, Dorcas?" She smiled, holding out both hands to Dorcas.

Dorcas chose Norma's left hand. "Oh, Mother. Norma gave me a piece

of her candy." Dorcas hurried to unwrap it. "Thank you, Norma," she said happily after taking her first bite.

"You are welcome," Norma replied as she took the wrapper off the candy for her little brother. "Here, Kevin. Do you want a piece of candy?" Kevin had a big smile for Norma too.

That evening while Norma dried the dishes for Mother, Mother said to her, "You seemed really happy when you shared your candy with Dorcas and Kevin."

"I was very happy," Norma agreed as she dried a plate.

"The Bible says that it is more blessed to give than to receive," Mother said, smiling. "You were happy when Sister Elaine gave you the candy, but you were very happy when you saw how happy Dorcas and Kevin were."

"We do not often have candy, so I wanted them to have some too," Norma said, smiling as she looked at Mother's happy face.

20.

Rosanna's Father

Rosanna smiled as she neatly cut around the red rose she had traced from Sister Ruth's pattern. She wanted her art project to look special because she was making it for Mother.

Sister Ruth walked up and down the aisles, checking on the children's work. Then she went to the chalkboard. She said, "On the front of your rose, I want you to print neatly

To Father and Mother

*With Love, From*_____

Where I have put this line, you may print your name."

Suddenly, Rosanna's smile faded. She did not look at the chalkboard anymore. She stared at her red rose instead. "I cannot write *To Father* on mine," she thought miserably. "I do not have a father."

Just then Sister Ruth walked by Rosanna's desk. She noticed Rosanna's sad face. "Rosanna," she said quietly, "you may write *To Mother* or *To Grandmother and Grandfather* on your rose. Do you know how to spell *Grandfather* and *Grandmother*?"

Rosanna nodded and smiled a little. Sister Ruth always seemed to know what to do.

The rest of the art period was spent putting glue on the ribbon and pasting

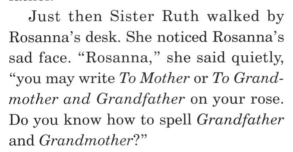

it to the rose.

Then it was time to do the cleaning duties. Rosanna checked the chart. "It is my turn to sweep the carpets," she thought. She pulled the long carpets outside the door. When she began sweeping, Sister Ruth joined her and helped her do the sweeping.

"Rosanna," Sister Ruth began kindly, "I did not want you to feel badly about not being able to write *Father* on your rose. You are no different from the rest of the children in our class. You and everyone else had a father at one time. Sometimes fathers and mothers die. Sometimes they are sick and cannot care for their children. Then God gives them a new father or mother.

"When your mother adopted you, God gave you a new mother. She loves you very much. Your new mother was never

married, so that is why you do not have
a new father."

Rosanna swept very carefully. She
was thinking about what Sister Ruth
had said. Mother had explained it to her
before.

Sister Ruth continued, "You know
Dwight, who will be in first grade next
year? His mother died. Now God gave
him a new mother, just as He gave you a
new mother. Do you understand?"

Rosanna nodded. "Mother says that
when Grandfather and Grandmother
come to live with us, then Grandfather
will be a father to both of us."

"That is right," Sister Ruth agreed.
"God is our Father too. Even if you do
not have a father at home, you can talk
to God. He is your heavenly Father."

Rosanna pulled the carpets back
inside. She was glad that Sister Ruth

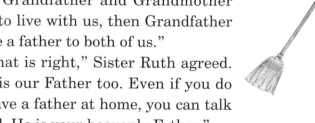

understood her. She smiled and prayed, "Thank You, God, for my mother and Grandfather and Grandmother. And thank You for Sister Ruth."

21

A Little Extra
Story Time

Marvin entered the classroom and placed his lunch box on the shelf. After a good-morning to Sister Elsie, who was busy at her desk, he raced to the Ping-Pong game in the next room.

Only a few minutes later, the bell rang and everyone in the class took his seat. For devotions that morning, they sang a few songs and then Sister Elsie stood by her desk to tell the story of Elisha's servant.

"Gehazi lied to Elisha when his master asked him if he had gone anywhere. He said that he had not gone away. But Elisha knew that Gehazi had gone down the road to talk to some men. God punished Elisha's servant for saying something that was not true." Sister Elsie was speaking in a serious voice.

"God does not want us to tell lies today either. And those who tell a lie must still be punished." Sister Elsie closed her Bible.

But instead of having prayer as she usually did, she talked some more to the children. "Yesterday I promised you that if everyone was finished with his arithmetic by lunchtime, I would read some extra in our storybook. Do you remember that?"

The children nodded their heads. Marvin was puzzled. "I wonder why she

asked that question."

Sister Elsie continued. "All of you said you were finished, so I read some extra pages from our storybook. Last evening when I was checking your papers, I was disappointed to find that one person was not done. On the bottom of the page, it said, 'I did not have time to finish this.'"

Marvin's heart pounded. "It wasn't me," he thought. "I remember that I finished mine." Marvin noticed that Dale looked sad.

Sister Elsie spoke quietly. "It is nice to have extra story time, but I do not want you to lie. Let's bow our heads for prayer."

Marvin thought, "Sister Elsie seems so sad."

Sister Elsie prayed, "Dear Lord, bless all the boys and girls here today. Help them to grow up to be men and women

who always speak the truth. In Jesus' Name. Amen."

After she had finished the prayer, Sister Elsie spoke again. "The one who lied has told an untruth to the whole class. He will need to be punished."

"Dale," Sister Elsie said, "come with me to the storage room. The rest of you may start with your lessons for today." Sister Elsie and Dale left the room.

Marvin opened his reading book. "I never ever want to tell a lie," he decided. "Dale would be happier if he had told the truth and had done without a little extra story time."

22

Anson Forgets

Anson was in second grade. He was doing his penmanship when Sister Ruth announced, "Recess time!" He closed his book and threw it into his desk. His pencil landed on top of his book, and his desk banged shut.

Anson loved recess time, and it did not seem long at all until it was time to go back to his work. When Sister Ruth called for math class, he had to dig under the pile of books to

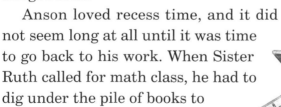

find his math book. That took extra time.

"Anson, what is your problem?" Sister Ruth asked while the others were waiting at the class table.

"I cannot find my book." Anson's answer was muffled because his head was behind his open desktop.

Sister Ruth came to Anson's desk. "I think too it would be hard to find a book in your desk," she said quietly. "Your desk is a mess."

A pile of books went sliding, and then out came Anson's head and down went Anson's desktop. He grabbed his pencil and took big steps to the table for class. He was happy he had found his book.

Fifteen minutes before school was over that day, Sister Ruth said, "It is time to put your books away. Today I have an announcement to make."

Papers rustled, desktops closed,

and soon everyone was ready for the announcement. Anson wondered what Sister Ruth would say next.

"We have a problem with messy desks. We want to be orderly in our classroom, as the Bible tells us to be. Take everything out of your desks, and wash them out with a damp cloth; then pile the biggest books at the bottom and the smallest at the top. Put your pencils and erasers beside your books or in your pencil cases."

Anson pulled books and papers and trash out of his desk. He put the trash into the wastebasket and the loose papers into his notebook. He put the books on a nice stack and returned the library book to the library. He put his pencils, eraser, and crayons in his pencil case. Then he wiped out his desk.

Next Anson stacked all his

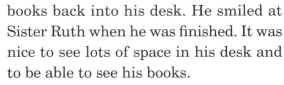

books back into his desk. He smiled at Sister Ruth when he was finished. It was nice to see lots of space in his desk and to be able to see his books.

"Now," said Sister Ruth when everyone was finished, "I hope we can keep our desks looking neater. I plan to check your desks every once in a while. If your desk is neat, you will get a little surprise. If your desk is messy, there will be nothing for you that day."

Big smiles spread around the room. Anson smiled too. He wanted one of Sister Ruth's surprises.

One day passed. Two days passed. "I wonder when Sister Ruth will check our desks," he thought. "I wish she would do it today because my desk is still looking nice."

Three days passed. Four days passed. On the fifth day when

Anson came to school, Beth was showing two Hershey Kisses to her friend Mary Ann. Mary Ann hurried to her desk. "I have two Hershey Kisses in my desk too," she squealed.

Anson walked slowly to his desk. He was not sure he would find candy in his desk, but, oh, how he hoped he would find some.

He opened his desk but could not find any candy. Instead he saw crayons that should have been in his pencil case. His math book was open on top of his pile of books. He saw three scattered papers that he had planned to take home. He had forgotten, and his desk was a mess again.

He closed his desk and looked sadly at Sister Ruth.

"You can try for the next surprise," Sister Ruth suggested. "I will

be checking your desks again."

Anson's sad eyes brightened. "I will try," he promised. And he did! The next time Sister Ruth checked his desk, it was nicely in order. This time the little surprise was a puppy eraser. How happy Anson was that he had had an orderly desk!

23

Arithmetic Perseverance

Seven-year-old James ran up the porch steps. He opened the screen door and called, "Mother, I'm home!"

"Hello, James." Mother smiled at James from where she was unpacking a big box. "How did everything go at school today?"

James's eyes shone. "I like this new school. I like having Sister Sarah for a teacher." But then he suddenly remembered something else. His eyes became

sad, and his smile went away. "But, Mother, our school in Pennsylvania was not at the same lesson in our arithmetic books as the school here in Tennessee."

Mother was concerned. "Did Sister Sarah send any papers home for you to do?"

"Yes," James sighed. "I counted the papers, and I am twenty papers behind the others. Sister Sarah said if I bring two papers home every evening to work on, I will be caught up with the other second graders in two weeks. That is a long time, isn't it?"

"Yes," Mother agreed, "two weeks is a while." Mother closed the box she had been unpacking and set it aside. "James, do you remember how you used to take Blackie for walks before we moved to Tennessee?" Mother asked.

They had moved only a few days

before, and Blackie had been James's favorite calf from the calf barn. James's smile returned, and his eyes did not look sad now. He looked at Mother. "Yes!"

Mother continued, "The first day you put a halter on Blackie he did not want to walk beside you. You kept on trying every day until finally he followed you around just like a pet."

"I had lots of fun with him after he walked beside me nicely," James commented. "But I had to work hard before that."

"You did a good job," Mother said. "You kept on trying and trying. We call that perseverance. The Bible calls it being diligent. Now you must also persevere with your arithmetic papers. Every evening after you have had your snack, take the two papers for that day and sit at Father's desk and work the

problems. After you have finished, you may go play."

James got off the couch slowly. "I'll try," he promised. He took his two papers into Father's office.

James worked faithfully and diligently. Every evening for ten school days, he took two arithmetic papers home from his second-grade arithmetic book. Every morning for ten school days, he handed Sister Sarah two neatly finished arithmetic papers.

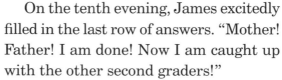

On the tenth evening, James excitedly filled in the last row of answers. "Mother! Father! I am done! Now I am caught up with the other second graders!"

"Good for you!" Father commended him with a smile.

"Good for you!" Mother smiled happily. "I knew you could do it."

24.

Aunt Barbara Too?

"Rosa! Regina!" Mother called. "Come here, please."

Rosa and Regina jumped up immediately. Their interesting game of Memory would have to wait until later.

The girls entered the kitchen. "Yes, Mother. You called us," Rosa said for both of them.

Mother smiled. "Aunt Barbara just called. She and Uncle Stephen need help to dig their potatoes this

afternoon. Would you girls like to go help them?"

"Oh, Mother, you know we want to go!" Rosa clapped her hands.

"I want to go too," Regina said eagerly.

"You must be careful on your walk over," Mother warned. "I know you often walk the short distance to Uncle Stephen's place, but you must call me when you get there."

"We will," the girls promised.

Happily they skipped down the little street. The ditches on each side of the street were filled with leaves that were falling from the big trees. Suddenly Regina exclaimed, "I have an idea! On the way home, let's gather pretty leaves."

"Yes, I want to do that too," Rosa agreed. "You could go on one side of the street, and I could go on the other. Then we could find more different kinds."

"Come in!" Aunt Barbara called when she heard the girls at the door.

"Come out!" Uncle Stephen called laughingly from the garden behind the house. He had heard the girls talking.

Soon Regina was picking up the big brown potatoes that Uncle Stephen had dug. She put them into a bushel basket. After Rosa had called Mother, she brought the wagon from the garage with another bushel basket to pick up more potatoes. It took a while to fill both bushel baskets. After both baskets were full, the girls pulled the wagon into the garage and helped Uncle Stephen unload them. After the girls washed their hands, Aunt Barbara gave them each a cookie and some lemonade.

"Thank you, Aunt Barbara!" both girls said. Soon it was time to leave.

"Good-bye, Aunt Barbara!"

Regina waved on her way out the door.

"Good-bye, and thank you so much for helping us!" Aunt Barbara stood on the porch as the girls went down the sidewalk. "Remember to stay on the same side of the street all the way home," she said. "There is not much traffic on this little street, but you must be careful."

Disappointed, Rosa turned to Regina. "I really wanted to find lots of leaves, but now Aunt Barbara said we must stay together. We could go on both sides of the street once Aunt Barbara goes into the house," she suggested, looking back at Aunt Barbara's porch.

"I guess we could." Regina sounded doubtful.

"Maybe we shouldn't." Rosa noticed that her sister was not too eager.

"I guess we shouldn't," Regina decided. "Father tells us we must obey

our teachers and ministers because the Bible says, 'Obey them that have the rule over you.' "

"I wonder if that means Aunt Barbara too," Rosa replied.

"We could ask Mother when we get home. But we had better stay together on this side of the street because Aunt Barbara told us to," Regina said.

Soon the girls were home. By the time they got home, their hands were full of pretty yellow, orange, and red leaves. Rosa and Regina laid their treasures on the table and spread them out. "We found lots of leaves even though we obeyed Aunt Barbara," Rosa said happily.

"Even though you obeyed Aunt Barbara?" Mother questioned. "What do you mean?"

So they told Mother what Aunt Barbara had said. "Mother, do

you really think we had to obey Aunt Barbara?" Rosa asked seriously. "She is not our mother."

"Yes, that verse means Aunt Barbara too," Mother agreed. "She was the person who was responsible for you when you were with her."

Regina and Rosa smiled. They were glad they had chosen to obey Aunt Barbara.

25.

Ellen's New Friend

Ellen followed Mother as they entered the church house. Mother chose to sit on a bench in the middle of the auditorium. They sat quietly, waiting for the service to begin.

The benches were filling up with more and more people. Then Ellen noticed a girl sitting with Sister Anna. "She doesn't usually come to church here," Ellen thought, looking at the girl who had dark   skin and

black, curly hair. "She is about my age," Ellen decided.

During the service, Ellen smiled a welcome to the new girl. "I wonder what her name is. I will ask her when we are dismissed." Ellen liked to have friends.

After Brother Paul led the closing prayer, Ellen smiled at the new girl. Then she looked at Mother.

"Remember to talk quietly to your friends," Mother reminded her.

"I will," Ellen promised.

Ellen walked slowly to the new girl. "My name is Ellen. What is your name?" she asked kindly.

"Vera." The new girl smiled a little.

"Come," Ellen invited Vera. "Let's go talk to the babies. My mother doesn't want me to ask the mothers to hold their babies, but I like to talk to them."

"Yes. Let's do that." Vera smiled a big smile now.

The two new friends walked down the side aisle together. "My sister has a tiny baby. She will let us look at her," Ellen suggested. "She is over here." Ellen led the way to her sister.

Ellen's sister smiled at Ellen's new friend. Then she sat on the bench so the girls could watch the tiny baby. Little Lisa Joy squirmed and stretched while the girls watched her.

"I like to watch tiny babies." Vera was excited. "But where I live some fathers and mothers do not care for their babies. Then a nurse comes and takes the baby to the hospital, where they take care of the baby."

"Oh, that is sad!" Ellen shuddered.

"Yes, it is," Ellen's sister sighed. "God loves every baby."

"I live in a big city in New York," Vera answered. "I came to stay with Jason and Anna's family for two weeks of summer vacation from the city."

"I am glad that you came to church," Ellen said thoughtfully. "I like to be your friend."

"You are kind to me," Vera answered. "I like to be your friend too."

Soon Mother came to tell Ellen that Father was ready to go. "Are you girls friends already?" she asked, smiling warmly at them.

"Yes, Mother." Ellen smiled happily. "Her name is Vera, and we are friends."

"I am glad. Hello, Vera," Mother said with a warm smile.

Then Ellen and her family went home. Ellen remembered her friend Vera for many years. Even though she did not see her often, she remembered

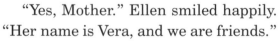

to pray for her sometimes. When Ellen was a mother, she was glad that she had been kind to a girl who was very different from herself.

26.

Good, Better, Best

Daniel put his third-grade reading workbook on Sister Janet's desk. "I think my work is all finished," he thought, smiling to himself. "I finished my math this morning. My social studies and spelling are finished too." He raised his hand.

"Yes, Daniel?" Sister Janet looked at him with a nod.

"What shall I do?" Daniel asked eagerly. Sometimes Sister Janet let him

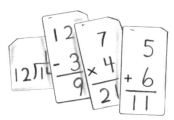

straighten up the bookshelves. Sometimes he flashed math facts for the first
graders. He liked to get done with his
work.

"Well . . ." Sister Janet thought a bit.
"I need someone to take the pictures off
the bulletin board. I think you can do
that if you work quietly. Put the pictures
on my desk and the staples in the wastebasket."

Daniel got the chair to stand on so
that he could reach the pictures. He
put the pictures on Sister Janet's desk
and the staples in the wastebasket. He
worked quietly. The rest of the children
were studying, and Sister Janet was
checking books at her desk.

Five minutes later, Sister Janet
announced, "Put your books
away." The children cleared their
desks and waited for Sister

Janet to dismiss them.

Sister Janet noticed their eagerness to go for recess. "You may go."

Daniel stepped down from the chair. "I am not finished yet," he told Sister Janet.

"You are doing fine," Sister Janet praised him. The rest of the children had left the room. Sister Janet quietly closed the schoolroom door.

"Daniel, I want to show you something." She opened his reading workbook. "Today your grade is 86 percent. That is not a bad grade. But I believe you could do better if you took a little more time."

Sister Janet pointed to a few misspelled words that she had circled. "You can check your reader to find how to spell those names. The answers to these questions are in your story. I like when

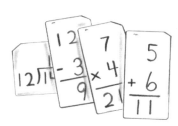

you help me with the bulletin board, but I would be happier if your grades were higher. Do you understand?"

Daniel nodded. "I will try," he promised.

"Good," said Sister Janet with a smile. "Schoolwork is easier for you than it is for some children, but you must still do your very best. Some children may not be able to get very many 100 percents in their reading, but I believe you could if you tried harder. You may go now."

Daniel dashed out the door to play with the others.

The next morning Daniel carefully read his reading story and searched his book for the answers. "It takes longer to do my reading if I make sure every answer is right," Daniel thought. "But Sister Janet thinks I can

get 100 percent, so I am going to try."

He finished his book a while later. He smiled at Sister Janet. "I tried to get 100 percent," he told her.

"I am glad," Sister Janet said, returning his smile. "God wants you to do your best."

Sister Janet was happy when she checked Daniel's book. Daniel was happy when he saw the grade in his book. He had gotten 100 percent because he had done his work carefully. Sister Janet needed to circle only one misspelled word.

For four days in a row, Daniel got 100 percent in his reading workbook.

"I am so glad," Sister Janet said quietly. "Keep it up."

Daniel smiled. He felt happy when he did his best.

27.

Pitch and Catch

"Sister Esther, may I go and play?" Stephen asked.

"Sister Esther, may I go too?" questioned Jason next.

"Sister Esther, I am finished with my chores now. May I go too?" Kenneth asked as he put his wet rag in the bucket.

The children at Mt. Zion School were doing their cleaning chores. Sister Esther checked to be sure the boys had cleaned properly. Then she said, "Yes, you may

go play until I ring the bell."

Kenneth hurried to the box for his ball and glove. He loved to play pitch and catch with Stephen and Jason. He dug through the box in the entry. "Where is my glove?" he wondered as Stephen and Jason went outside.

Just then Kenneth looked up and noticed that Jonathan was sweeping the entry. "I should help Jonathan," Kenneth thought as he pulled his glove out from beneath the other gloves. "But I really want to play pitch and catch too."

Hesitating at the door, Kenneth saw that Stephen and Jason were already pitching the ball back and forth. Then he looked back at Jonathan again, sweeping all by himself.

"I know what I will do," Kenneth decided. "I will help Jonathan first; then I can play pitch and catch. I think

Jonathan would like that."

He grabbed a broom from the closet and began sweeping. Jonathan got a big smile on his face when he saw that he had some help. "Thank you, Kenneth, for helping me. I still have a lot to sweep."

Kenneth smiled as he kept right on sweeping.

When Sister Esther put her broom away, she noticed that Kenneth was helping Jonathan. "Thank you, Kenneth, for helping Jonathan," she praised quietly.

Kenneth smiled again. He was glad that he had made Sister Esther and Jonathan happy.

"We are finished!" Jonathan announced a little later. "Thank you!"

"You're welcome," Kenneth replied as he once more grabbed his glove and flew outside to join Stephen and Jason. He had only a few minutes to play until

the bell rang, but he felt happy inside
because he had done what he knew was
the right thing to do.

28

Aunt Rose Makes
Tomato Soup

Phoebe was especially happy because God had given their family a baby boy. Phoebe had two brothers and one sister. Now they were happy for another baby boy.

"Mother, I am so glad that you and baby James are finally home from the hospital." Phoebe smiled at Mother, who was rocking baby James.

"I am very happy to be home

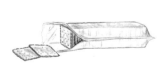

with my family again," Mother replied. "Two days seemed like a long time when I could not see you. Are you finished drying dishes for Aunt Rose?" Mother questioned.

"Yes, Mother. The dishes are finished," Phoebe answered. "I think Aunt Rose went out to pick the tomatoes."

"I want you to be Aunt Rose's helper until I feel stronger," Mother instructed. "Please go help Aunt Rose bring the tomatoes to the house. Then tell her to make tomato soup for lunch today. I want to rest until lunchtime."

"All right, Mother. I will help her, and I will tell her to make tomato soup for lunch." Then Phoebe sped out to the garden.

All morning Aunt Rose cut up tomatoes. Phoebe put them into the kettle to cook. When it was lunchtime, Aunt Rose

said, "Will you please set the table? I am
making tomato soup."

"Good." Phoebe smiled. "I really like
tomato soup. Mother makes it often."

"I am glad you like it," Aunt Rose
said. "Would you go call Mother now?
Tell her that lunch is ready. Remember
to go quietly."

Soon Mother, Aunt Rose, Phoebe,
and the other children sat at the table.
Mother asked God to bless the food.
Then Phoebe carefully dipped one big
dipper full of soup into her bowl. Aunt
Rose dipped soup for the other children.

Phoebe crushed some crackers into
her soup. She stirred it round and round
because it was so hot. After a few bites,
Phoebe looked at Mother. "I like your
tomato soup better than this," she told
Mother.

Mother looked sadly at Phoebe.

Then she looked at Aunt Rose. "I think this soup is delicious."

Mother excused the children when they were finished eating. "Phoebe, come with me," Mother said quietly.

Phoebe pushed her chair back and slowly followed Mother into the living room. Somehow she thought she knew what Mother wanted.

"Phoebe," Mother said quietly, "it was not kind of you to say that you like my soup better. Aunt Rose cooks differently than I do, but that is because her mother taught her that way. The soup was really very good, but it did have a different spice in it than mine usually does."

Phoebe looked at her bare feet. She was sorry for what she had said.

Mother continued, "Maybe Aunt Rose feels sad inside because of what you said. I want you to come with me

and tell her you are sorry for saying that."

"Oh, Mother!" Phoebe was in tears now. "Must I really do that? I am so sorry."

"Yes, Phoebe." Mother was firm. "The Bible way to fix our mistakes is to say we are sorry. Come."

Phoebe followed Mother to the kitchen. There, she said, "Aunt Rose, I am sorry." Then she burst into tears.

Aunt Rose knew what Phoebe meant. She hugged her and said, "It is all right now. You are forgiven."

Then Phoebe felt better. She would remember not to say anything bad about the food that Aunt Rose cooked for them while Mother was resting.

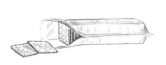

29.

Ruby Describes

"Peas to shell! Peas to shell!" sang Mother as she carried two buckets of green peas to the porch. Wearily she sat on the lawn chair and rubbed her back.

Carl, Glenda, and Ruby came running, leaving their toys behind. "What can I do?" asked Carl.

"Please bring four bowls to the porch," Mother said as she got up again. "Glenda, you may bring chairs to sit on."

"What shall I do?" Ruby asked.

"You may help Carl carry the bowls out here, dear," Mother answered. "I will get a box for the hulls."

Soon many hands were reaching into the buckets of peas to fill their bowls. *Snapity-snap. Snapity-snap.* Little round peas ran into the corners to hide. *Snapity-snap. Snapity-snap.*

"Mother, let's play the guessing game," Carl suggested eagerly. "We played it the last time we shelled peas. Remember?"

Mother nodded. "Carl, you may be the first one to describe something."

Carl smiled. He looked all around the porch. Finally he said, "I am thinking about something white. It touches the ground. It is made of wood."

Glenda looked around. "Is it neighbor Joe's fence?" she quickly asked.

"Right!" Carl smiled. "Now it is your

turn to describe something."

Glenda was ready. "I am thinking about something small and silver."

"Small and silver?" Mother asked. "Is it the wagon wheel?"

"No." Glenda shook her head excitedly.

"Tell us more about it," Carl begged.

Glenda smiled. "It has black letters on it."

"The mailbox!" Carl exclaimed.

"Yes," Glenda said, smiling. "Now it is your turn again."

"I can never guess the right thing," Ruby said sadly. "I wish I could think that quickly."

Carl was thinking about something to describe. He was also thinking about something else: "Ruby is lots smaller than I am."

"Ruby, would you like to take my turn this time?" he asked kindly.

"Oh yes!" Ruby's smile got bigger and bigger until she giggled. "Thank you!" she said as she looked around to see what she could describe to the others.

Mother's tired smile made Carl feel good inside. He knew he had pleased Mother by sharing his turn with Ruby.

Ruby looked at the grass. Then she said, "I see something green. It is little."

"Is it grass?" Carl guessed quickly.

"Yes." Ruby laughed.

From that time on, Carl enjoyed the game even more. It took a long time to shell two buckets of peas, but the time seemed short as they played the guessing game. Ruby enjoyed the game too, because sometimes Carl let her have a turn.

30.

Sunshine Does Not Understand

"It's four-thirty," eight-year-old Curtis announced, jumping up from the recliner in the living room. Putting his book back on the shelf, he said to himself, "Time to chore." He put on his barn jacket and left the house.

As Curtis entered the heifer barn, he greeted the eighteen animals. "Hello," he said as he walked slowly toward the feed sack. "Are you hungry tonight?"

"One, two, three," Curtis counted the scoops of feed aloud. "Four, five, six, seven, eight, nine. That's all you get tonight." He chuckled as he watched them hungrily dig into their feed.

Then his eyes saw a commotion at the other end of the feed trough. "Sunshine! What shall I do with you?" Curtis sighed as he watched Sunshine butting in here and there, trying to find the most feed and the best spot to eat it.

Finally Curtis ran to find Father. "Father, can you come to the heifer barn?" he panted. "I have a problem with Sunshine. She is so greedy when I feed the heifers."

"I'll come and see," Father said, laying down the scoop he had in his hand.

"See, Father," Curtis said, pointing to Sunshine. "She is so busy moving around that she still did not get much to eat.

Soon all the feed will be gone."

"Well," said Father thoughtfully, "I suppose there is not much we can do about it. It is her own fault if she does not get much to eat. There—now she is staying at one place in the line."

"Yes, but now there is not much feed left," Curtis said, frowning.

"You are right," Father agreed. "But it cannot be helped. Sunshine reminds me of people who are selfish. They think if they can get the best things in life, and the most, they will be happy. In the end, they are not as well off as other people who are willing to give the best to others, because God blesses a cheerful giver."

Curtis sat on a bag of feed as he and Father watched the heifers licking up the last of the feed with their long tongues. "I do not want to be like Sunshine," he said. "I want to share with others."

"We all want to be like that," Father agreed. "You can share your toys and books with your friends when they visit us. You can share many things with your brothers and sisters. Then you will be happy. But Sunshine really doesn't understand. She is just an animal."

Then Father and Curtis together fed hay to the animals.

31.

Thank You, God, for Big Brothers

Six-year-old Edward pulled his little red wagon under the big maple tree in the lawn. Suddenly he heard a roar above him in the sky. He shaded his eyes with his hand so that he could see better.

"A jet," Edward thought. "What a trail of smoke it is making as it goes along in the sky."

Edward sat on his wagon and cupped his head in his hands. He was thinking.

"Just last week, big brother Mark left the airport on one of those big jets. He flew many, many miles away. That is hard to understand."

He looked at the airplane again. It looked so tiny up in the sky. But Edward knew that it was very big, because he had seen those big airplanes at the airport last week.

And now Mark was far away. Edward got up from the wagon and slowly went to find Mother. "Mother," he began, "I miss Mark so much. I wish that he would not have gone away in that big airplane."

Mother smiled at Edward. "Father and I miss Mark too. But we must remember what Mark told us the evening he left. Mark said he feels God is telling him to go to help the poor children whose fathers and

mothers cannot care for them."

Mother continued to explain. "In Honduras, the children need someone to love them. So Mark went to help take care of those children. We can pray for Mark, you know."

Edward nodded his head. "Before Mark left, I promised him I would pray for him every day. I do that before I go to bed at night."

"That is good," Mother said. "I am sure that would make Mark happy."

That night, before Edward went to bed, he knelt on his little green rug. "Dear God," he prayed, "thank You for my family. Thank You for my big brother. Be with Mark in Honduras, where he cares for the little children. In Jesus' Name. Amen."

Many months passed by. Every day Edward prayed for

Mark. Finally one day big brother Mark flew on another airplane. This time he came home to live with his family again. "Thank You, God, for my big brother," Edward prayed that night when he went to bed. "Thank You that Mark is home again."

32.

The Damaged Bible

"Father, my Bible is so worn out." Frieda showed her black Bible to Father. "I would like to have a new one."

Father took Frieda's Bible in his hands. "Well," he said, "we will have to see. Mother and I are trying not to buy more than we have to for a few months, because of our hospital bills. Do you think you can make do with this Bible for a while yet?"

Frieda was disappointed as she laid

her Bible back on the shelf. "I will try,"
she said sadly.

Father was thoughtful as he and
Mother drove to town later that week.
"Frieda really does need a new Bible,"
he said. "Her old Bible is coming apart."

"Yes," Mother agreed. "But it is one
of those things that can wait. I believe
the Lord will provide. He is always
faithful."

"You are right, Mother. But I want to
stop at the bookstore and check prices
on the Bibles today," Father said as they
neared town.

"Can I help you, sir?" Mrs. Porter, the
lady at the counter, asked.

"Yes. I am checking prices today on
your children's Bibles," Father replied.
"Our daughter needs a new Bible, and
we plan to buy her one, but I do not
think we will buy it today."

Mrs. Porter showed Father the different Bibles that she had. "I think we will buy this one when we come back later," Father said at last. "We must be going now. Thank you."

"Oh, but I have a Bible just like that one, back here," Mrs. Porter said, walking behind the counter. "It is damaged a little on the cover, so it will not sell. You may take it for your daughter if you want it."

Father took the Bible in his hands. "Thank you," he said. "It doesn't look that bad to me."

"No, it isn't," she agreed. "But most people will not buy Bibles that are not perfect."

"I want to pay you something for it." Father reached for his wallet. "This Bible will be used a lot."

"No." Mrs. Porter firmly shook her

head. "I want to give it to you."

"Thank you," Father and Mother said as they smiled and left the store with the new Bible.

"Won't Frieda be surprised?" Mother said happily as she stepped into the van.

And Frieda really was surprised and pleased when Father handed her the Bible. "But, Father, you told me I would probably need to wait a while," Frieda said in surprise.

"I did not buy it, Frieda. The Lord provided it for you. It is damaged a little bit, so Mrs. Porter gave it to me for you."

Frieda held her Bible close. "I am so glad for a new Bible. Thank you, Father."

"You are welcome." Father was pleased to make Frieda happy. "But we must be sure to thank the Lord for it. The Lord saw your need, so He worked

it out for Mrs. Porter to give it to me today."

That night when Frieda went to bed, she knelt beside her bed and prayed, "Thank You, God, for my new Bible. Thank You!"

33

The One Side

$$\overset{2}{\cancel{3}}0$$
$$-\ \underline{17}$$
$$\ \ 13$$

Nine-year-old Vernon closed his arithmetic book. "My lesson is finished," he
thought happily as he put his book away.
"That was fun!"

Vernon looked at his third-grade
friend. Surprised, he looked again.
"Why, James is only on the first
page," he thought.

Just then James raised his
hand. Sister Mabel walked to his
desk. Vernon heard James say,

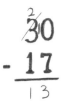

"I need help. I don't understand this lesson."

Vernon pulled out a puzzle book that Mother had sent to school with him. Sister Mabel had said he could do it in his spare time. Carefully he searched for the answers and neatly filled in the big blanks.

When he paused for a bit, he noticed that Sister Mabel was explaining the lesson to James again.

That evening while Vernon dried the dishes for Mother, he talked to her. "Today in school we learned something new again. It was called borrowing. I really liked doing it."

Question marks filled his voice as he continued. "But, Mother, why didn't James understand his lesson? It wasn't hard at all."

Mother was quiet for a moment as she

washed a few more dishes. "Vernon," she finally said, "God makes each person a little different. Some people can do certain things a lot easier than other people can.

"James is one who finds arithmetic a hard subject. Sister Mabel is trying to help him understand it step by step. If he keeps on trying, he will likely understand it soon," Mother explained.

"I wish that James would do his work faster," Vernon said sadly. "Then we could have more fun in school. He hardly ever has any spare time."

"That is true," Mother agreed, putting more plates on the rack for Vernon to dry. "But I believe James is trying. Sister Mabel and James's parents are happy because James keeps trying to do good work. One more thing, Vernon. You must

$$
\begin{array}{r}
\overset{2}{\cancel{3}}0 \\
-\ 17 \\
\hline
1\ 3
\end{array}
$$

always be kind to James. Never laugh at him if he doesn't understand his work."

"I want to be kind," Vernon said thoughtfully. "I like James for my friend."

"God made our minds," Mother said. "We want to thank Him, whether things are hard or easy for us."

34.

The Other Side

James listened carefully while Sister Mabel explained the new arithmetic lesson. After class he turned his book to the right lesson. "Borrowing looks so hard," he thought. "But I must try.

"I know that I need to cross out this number." James continued studying the first problem. "And I must put a number that is one less on top of it. But now what do I do?" James tried another problem, but it did not work out either.

Finally he raised his hand. Sister Mabel walked to his desk. "I don't know how to do these problems," he said sadly.

"I will explain it to you again," Sister Mabel said kindly. She pointed to the 6 that was above the 7. "The 6 is less than the 7, so you must run over here to the neighbors and borrow a number to make this enough. Now, what number do you have?"

James's eyes brightened. "Sixteen," he said.

"Yes," answered Sister Mabel. "Now what is 16 minus 7?"

"Nine," James said with a smile.

"Right again!" Sister Mabel answered. "Now do you know how to finish this problem?"

"Yes, I do." James nodded. Then he noticed that his friend Vernon was working in a puzzle book. "Oh, how I wish

that I could do arithmetic that quickly," James thought as he copied the next problem. "Vernon is always finished first."

That evening James found his mother cooking supper. "Mother," he began, "today in arithmetic we learned something new again. Something about getting something from the neighbors."

"Was it called borrowing?" Mother had to smile.

"Yes, that is it," James replied. "It took me a long time to do it. I tried and tried, but I think I got some wrong anyway. But Vernon does his work so fast. It is easy for him. I wish I could get done so fast."

Mother said, "The Lord makes every child different. The Bible says that God gives different gifts to different people. Vernon seems to learn very quickly."

"But I would like to do puzzles in school too." James put the silverware by the plates.

"James, I know that it takes extra work for you to get good grades in school. But Sister Mabel and Father and I are pleased with how you keep on trying. Maybe someday you can work puzzles in school, but for now you must be content to study extra hard so that you can go on to fourth grade next year."

Mother cut the lettuce for the salad and then added, "I am sure that you and Vernon can be friends even though God has made you different."

"Yes, Mother, we are friends!" James smiled.

35.

Working for Money

"Mother! Mother!" Samuel raced into
the kitchen. "I just now noticed that
neighbor Raymond and his children are
picking up stones in the field out here.
May I please go and help them?"

Mother thought a bit. "I will call his
wife, Ellen, and see if Brother Raymond
needs your help," Mother said.

After finishing the telephone call,
Mother smiled at Samuel's eager face.
"Ellen says that Brother Raymond would

be happy for your help anytime."

"I am glad," Samuel said eagerly. "I am glad that I can go. Good-bye, Mother."

"Be careful," Mother called after him as he hurried out the door and across the lawn to the field next to their driveway.

Samuel ran across the strip of grass and into the soft brown soil of the newly tilled field. As he neared the tractor and wagon, an idea popped into his mind. "Maybe if I work really hard today, Brother Raymond will pay me some money." Samuel was happy with that thought.

"Here comes another helper," Brother Raymond welcomed Samuel. "We are glad for your help to pick up some of these many stones."

Samuel threw his first stone onto the wagon. He worked quickly. "If I want some money, I will have to work very

fast," he thought as he picked up many more stones.

Brother Raymond's children were tired of walking across the big field. After a while Samuel was tired too, but he tried not to slow down. He heaved a big stone onto the wagon. Then Brother Raymond said, "This load is full enough. Samuel, you may go home now, and we will take this load to the barn where we are filling in a ditch. Thank you so much for your help. You worked hard."

"Good-bye!" Samuel waved as he walked toward his house. Slowly he crossed the lawn and entered the house. Oh, how he wished that Brother Raymond had given him some money to put into his bank.

Mother noticed Samuel's sad face right away. "Are you tired?" she asked kindly.

"No, not too much," Samuel said.

"But I was hoping Brother Raymond would pay me for helping him, so I worked really hard. But he just said 'thank you' when I came home."

"Oh, Samuel!" Mother was surprised. "Father and I do not expect Brother Raymond to pay you when you help him work on his farm. Maybe when you are older you can earn some money, but you are too little now."

"I don't like being too little!" Samuel exclaimed. "I want to be big and work for people and get money."

"I know," Mother said. "When I was a little girl, I wanted to get paid for helping someone mow their lawn one day. I will tell you what Grandmother told me when I came home that day."

Samuel smiled, thinking about Mother being a little girl. "What did Grandmother tell you?" he asked.

"Why, she said that I would get paid with happiness at being able to help someone who had a need. She said that was worth more than money," Mother told her son.

"And, Mother, was it?" Samuel wanted to know.

"It really was, Samuel. I learned in the many years since that Grandmother was right, because that is what the Bible says too. 'It is more blessed to give than to receive.'"

"Well, I guess the next time I help Brother Raymond, I'll work hard for happiness instead of for money," Samuel decided. "Maybe when I am big, I can tell my boys what you told me."

"Maybe you can." Mother smiled at that thought.